TO THE SHOW

First published 1985 by
Deans International Publishing
Copyright © 1985 Victoria House Publishing Ltd.
This edition published 1989 by
Colour Library Books Ltd,
Godalming, Surrey, England.
ISBN 0 86283 660 3

Printed in the German Democratic Republic

LITTLE SQUIRREL'S
BEDTIME
STORIES

Written by Lis Taylor
Illustrated by Colin Petty

Colour Library Books

Contents

LITTLE
SQUIRREL'S
BEDTIME
STORIES

Little Squirrel's Pond

Little Squirrel had always wanted a pond.

"It would look lovely in the garden," she told Mr Squirrel.

"But it would be very hard work making a pond here," he told her. "We'd need an awful lot of water to fill it up."

So Little Squirrel had given up the idea of a pond and when Mr Squirrel built her a new sand pit she forgot about the pond altogether.

"Do you want to play in my sandpit?" she asked Little Mouse and Ricky Fox one day at school.

They thought that sounded fun and hurried home after school to ask their mummies. Soon the three of them were busy making sandcastles and digging away.

"I'm going to see if I can dig to the middle of the Earth," said Little Mouse. "I want to find out what it's like."

"Don't be silly!" said Little Squirrel. "You'll never get to the middle. It would take years and years!"

But Little Mouse kept on digging until she had quite disappeared into the deep hole she had made.

"I think she really does mean to keep digging until she gets to the middle," said Ricky with a laugh.

Just then there was a little cry from Little Mouse down the hole and she was swept into the air on a big jet of water.

"Ouch!" she squeaked as she landed with a bump. She jumped up and danced around. "I've done it, I've done it! I've dug to the middle of the Earth!" she cried.

"But look at all the water!" cried Little Squirrel. "It's filling up the sandpit. What are we going to do?"

She ran inside to tell Mr Squirrel that Little Mouse had dug to the middle of the Earth and that it was made of water. Mr Squirrel smiled quietly and said he would come and have a look.

By the time they got back the sandpit was nearly full and the water was only bubbling gently.

"You haven't dug to the middle of the Earth, Little Mouse," explained Mr Squirrel. "You've hit an underground spring. It's a place where a stream runs under the ground."

"How are we going to dry out the sandpit?" asked Ricky.

"I don't think we can," said Mr Squirrel. "That spring will keep bubbling up for ever now you've dug down to it—so it looks as though you've got the pond you wanted after all, Little Squirrel!"

The Birthday Seeds

Little Squirrel was visiting Grandpa Squirrel. He lived in a tall beech tree at the edge of the wood and spent most of his time working in his garden. He grew lovely big vegetables and beautiful flowers.

Little Squirrel was helping to plant seeds. She had sown a row of carrots and a row of cabbages while Grandpa planted peas and beans. When they had finished they went inside for a hot cup of acorn coffee and some fresh sunflower buns.

"Mmmm!" said Little Squirrel, biting into her third bun. "I like these better than any other buns!"

Grandpa laughed and then said, "I've got a birthday present for you." He dug into his pocket and pulled out a packet of seeds.

"But my birthday isn't for months!" said Little Squirrel.

"If you plant these now they'll be ready just in time," explained Grandpa. "You'd better plant them here. There isn't enough sunshine in the woods where you live."

So Little Squirrel planted her seeds and every week when she visited Grandpa and Grandma she went to look at them. For a long time nothing happened. Then little green shoots appeared and they grew and grew until they were taller than anything else in the garden.

Big buds appeared at the top of the stems and, at last, big yellow flowers opened out.

"Sunflowers! How lovely!" cried Little Squirrel. "But they are too early for my birthday."

Grandpa shook his head. "Your birthday present isn't ready yet," he said.

Little Squirrel didn't understand.

Soon it was Little Squirrel's birthday. The sunflowers were quite dead now. Their yellow heads had drooped and Little Squirrel was very puzzled about her present.

As she walked into the kitchen Grandpa came to meet her with a basket.

"Look," he said, pointing at the dead sunflowers. "What can you see?"

Little Squirrel looked carefully. "Seeds! Sunflower seeds!" she cried.

"That's right," said Grandpa. "There are enough seeds here to make your favourite buns for at least a year!"

And what was more, Grandma had baked a big batch of sunflower buns for Little Squirrel's birthday tea!

The Eggcup Game

"Let's play the Eggcup Game!" said Little Bunny.

"How do you play?" asked Little Mouse and Little Squirrel.

"Easy," said Little Owl. "You have to get as many things as possible into an eggcup."

"Right," said Little Bunny. "Everybody find an eggcup and try to fill it up. We'll meet back here in half an hour."

They all scampered off in different directions, but were soon back at Little Bunny's house.

"I've got five things!" exclaimed Little Squirrel, tipping out a sycamore seed, a pebble, a cherry stone, a dandelion leaf and a beetle (which ran away at once).

Little Mouse had four things and Little Owl had seven.

"I've won," boasted Little Bunny.

"How many have you got?" they all asked.

"I don't know, I can't count them all," he said, emptying out his eggcup that was full to the brim with poppy seeds! He had taken them from his mother's jar in the kitchen.

But Little Bunny didn't win, because, as Little Owl explained, all the things in the eggcup must be different.

The Party Dress

Every summer there was a grand party in Hollyholt. All the trees were decorated with flowers and lit by glow-worms. The Rambling Mousekins came with their flutes and fiddles and there was dancing until dawn—or until they all fell asleep.

As the day for this year's party drew near Little Squirrel got excited. She tried on her special party dress.

"Breathe in a bit, dear," said Mrs Squirrel, as she tried to do up the buttons. "It's no good. You've grown out of it. And there's no time to order any cloth from Mrs Spider so I can't make you a new one. You'll just have to wear your everyday dress."

Little Squirrel was miserable. She ran out of the house and didn't stop until she reached the stream. Tears rolled down her face and she sniffed unhappily.

"Whatever's the matter with you?" asked Mrs Duck, who was waddling up the bank.

Little Squirrel explained and Mrs Duck said, "Come with me." She led her back to her cosy little house in the reeds.

"Now let's see what we've got," said Mrs Duck, opening a big, wooden chest in the corner.

Little Squirrel was amazed to see all the feathers that spilled out of it—blue ones, green ones, beautiful rusty brown ones, fluffy ones, long shiny ones—all sorts.

"Which colours do you like best?" asked Mrs Duck, taking out her tape to measure Little Squirrel. "You'll be the only one at the party in a feather dress I should think."

Little Squirrel chose blue and green feathers. She helped Mrs Duck sew them all together. It was quite easy really, once you knew how.

At last the dress was ready.

"Try it on," said Mrs Duck. "There's a nice big mirror outside my door," she laughed, pointing at the stream.

"Oh! It's . . . it's beautiful! Thank you

ever so much, Mrs Duck," said Little Squirrel as she danced around on the bank, looking at herself in the water.

It was the best party Little Squirrel could remember. She was chosen as Woodland Princess for the evening and she danced and danced in her feathery dress until she fell asleep and Mr Squirrel carried her home.

The Coconut Cake Competition

One day, Little Squirrel and Tootie Owl ran down to Mrs Badger's shop to buy some sweets and were surprised to find the shop piled high with cardboard boxes.

"What's in all these boxes, Mrs Badger?" asked Little Squirrel.

"Coconut!" said Mrs Badger, sounding tired. "I meant to order three boxes, but by mistake I ordered thirty. There's enough here to keep the whole village going for years!"

"Poor Mrs Badger," said Tootie, as they sat outside eating dandelion sherbet. "I wish we could help."

"I think we can," said Little Squirrel.

The next day there was quite a crowd on the green, all reading a poster that had been fixed to the biggest tree:

COCONUT CAKES COMPETITION
NEXT SATURDAY
EXCITING PRIZES FOR THE BEST CAKES

"I think it's going to work!" whispered Little Squirrel to Tootie.

They rushed back to Mrs Badger's and the shop was packed. Everyone was buying coconut. Mrs Badger couldn't believe it until Little Squirrel explained, and she was so pleased that she rushed around looking for prizes. Between them they decided on a big bunch of flowers for first prize, and some fudge for the runners-up.

COCONUT CAKES
COMPETITION
NEXT SATURDAY
EXCITING PRIZES
OR THE BEST CAKES

Little Squirrel told the whole story to her mummy.

"What a clever idea," said Mrs Squirrel. "I could make some coconut pyramids. Can you pop down to Mrs Badger's for some coconut?"

But when Little Squirrel asked Mrs Badger for the coconut, Mrs Badger started to laugh.

"Goodness me," she chuckled, "this is my last packet. Now I'll have to order some more!"

Making Ginger Beer

Every once in a while Mrs Owl made a batch of ginger beer. This time Little Owl had asked if he could help, so he was busily stirring everything in a big bowl while Mrs Owl measured out the right amount of sugar.

"We put the sugar straight into the bottles," she explained. "One teaspoonful in each bottle. It must be exactly a teaspoonful, no more, or it will be too fizzy. Will you put it in while I go and fetch the labels?"

So Little Owl put the sugar in the bottles.

"I *do* like sweet, fizzy ginger beer," he thought. "And I'm sure a little bit extra won't do any harm."

So he put an extra teaspoonful in every bottle!

They filled up the bottles and stuck on the labels. Then they carried them out to the shed and left them there.

"They should be ready to drink in about a week," said Mrs Owl, as she closed the door.

Little Owl was impatient. He could hardly wait a week to try the ginger beer and when, at last, the week was up he wanted to

fetch a bottle for breakfast!

"Just be patient," said Mrs Owl. "We'll try some later."

As she was speaking there was a loud pop outside in the garden.

"What was that?" asked Mrs Owl, looking through the window. As she looked there was another pop, and another, and then several all at once. They all ran out into the garden, but there was nothing to see.

Then Tootie called, "Look!" and pointed at the shed.

Something was trickling under the door. Mrs Owl opened it and there were all the ginger beer bottles, corks popped all over the place, with little fountains of ginger beer pouring from each bottle.

"That's never happened before," said Mrs Owl, looking puzzled. "Well, we'll have to drink it *all* straight away. Little Owl and Tootie, I think you'd better invite your friends round for a ginger beer party this morning."

Mrs Owl never found out why the bottles all popped and Little Owl didn't tell her why the ginger beer was so fizzy. After all, it was fun having a ginger beer party!

19

New Roller Skates for Little Mouse

Little Mouse was looking sad.

"What's the matter?" asked Little Squirrel.

"My feet have grown," moaned Little Mouse.

"What's wrong with that? Everybody grows."

"But I've grown too big for my roller skates. Daddy says I'll have to wait until Christmas for some more and that's ages. I've seen some lovely ones in Hollyholt Stores but they'll be gone before Christmas, I'm sure."

"Don't worry," said Little Squirrel. "Why don't you come blackberrying with Mummy, Daddy and me? That might cheer you up."

Mrs Squirrel gave them each a big basket and they set off to the blackberry patch. Mr Squirrel hummed a little song as they walked along:

> Blackberry pies and blackberry jam,
> How happy I am, how happy I am
> To pick blackberries, blackberries all the time.

Soon they were all singing it and Little Mouse started to feel a lot better.

"My goodness," said Mrs Squirrel. "Look at all those berries! It must mean a cold winter ahead."

They all began picking, humming the Blackberry Song, and the

time went by very quickly. They didn't notice how full their baskets were getting. By the time Mrs Squirrel called them to go home, all the baskets were piled high.

"I'm sure we've picked more than enough," said Mr Squirrel, looking at all the juicy berries. "These will make pots of jam!"

He was right. That afternoon they all helped Mrs Squirrel make blackberry jam—and soon the windowsill and both tables were covered with jars. They wondered what to do with them all.

"I know!" shouted Little Squirrel. "Let's take them down to Hollyholt Stores."

Mrs Badger was pleased to see them. Little Squirrel and Little Mouse staggered up to her, pushing a wheelbarrow packed with jars of jam.

"I'd be glad to take it off your hands," she said, "but I'd like to give you something for all your hard work."

Then, to their surprise, she handed Little Squirrel a fine skipping rope with blue handles—and Little Mouse the roller skates from the window.

"I didn't know blackberrying could be such fun!" laughed Little Mouse as she skated home.

Little Squirrel and the Rosy Apples

Little Squirrel and Mrs Squirrel had been picking apples and they had a big basketful. Little Squirrel was very fond of apples and so was Grandpa Squirrel, so she thought she would take some over to him. She chose some small, rosy ones, tied them in a cloth, and popped them into her basket.

She had to pass the shop to get to Grandpa's and she thought

she would pop in and give an apple to Mrs Badger, who was always so kind.

Mr Mole was in the shop too, so she gave them each an apple, then walked on until she came to the Bunnies' house, where baby Bunnikins was playing in the garden.

"Would you like an apple?" she asked.

Bunnikins couldn't talk much, but she nodded her head up and down.

"Is it all right for her to have one?" Little Squirrel asked Mrs Bunny.

"Yes, dear," said Mrs Bunny. "If I cut it up small. They look very tasty." So Mrs Bunny had one too and so did Little Bunny and his brother Benny.

Little Squirrel set off again. She was starting to feel hungry as it was getting near to tea time.

"It won't matter if I have just one apple," she thought and she reached into the basket. Mmm! It tasted very good.

Grandma and Grandpa were pleased to see her and Grandpa was even more pleased when she told him what she had in her basket. She handed it to him and he carefully untied the cloth.

"Ha ha!" laughed Grandpa. "That's a good joke." The basket was empty!

"It wasn't a joke," said Little Squirrel, starting to cry. "The basket was full when I set out, but I gave one apple to Timmy Mouse and one to Mrs Badger and—and to lots of other people too. I must have given them all away."

"Never mind," said Grandma, putting her arm round Little Squirrel. "It was very kind of you to give apples to everyone."

"I've got a good idea," said Grandpa, jumping up. "Since we haven't got any apples, I think we should have our tea and then go blackberry picking. Little Squirrel deserves a treat—and there will be plenty of blackberries for everyone!"

The Village Show

Grandpa Squirrel was picking his best marrow for the Holyholt show. For weeks he had been carefully looking after it and watching it grow and grow.

"Just look," he said to Little Squirrel. "Isn't that the best marrow you've ever seen?"

They packed it carefully into a basket and set off for the show.

By the time they reached the village green it was quite crowded. Most of their friends were there, carrying baskets of vegetables or homemade jam and cakes. The judges were sitting at the tables under the chestnut tree trying all the bottles of dandelion wine that were in the competition.

"Morning," called Grandpa to Mr Bunny. "How is your dandelion wine doing?"

"Not too well. One of the judges pulled a face when he tried it. What are you showing?"

"The best marrow in the world," said Grandpa proudly, holding up his basket. "What do you think of that?"

"Pretty good," said Mr Bunny, "but I would look out for Mr Weasel's marrow. I've heard it's a whopper!"

Mr Weasel was standing all by himself at the far side of the village green. He was holding a big bag that was carefully zipped up so that no one could see what was inside.

"Oh dear," said Grandpa Squirrel. "It's certainly a big bag. . . ."

The judges called for marrows. Grandpa Squirrel went over with the others and they all put their marrows carefully on the tables in front of the judges. Grandpa looked at all the marrows. Mr Shrew's was pretty big, but not quite as big as his. Grandpa smiled.

Then Mr Weasel unzipped his bag and lifted out the fattest, longest, greenest marrow that Grandpa had ever seen!

"I don't believe it," said Grandpa, shaking his head.

"First prize to Mr Weasel, second prize to Grandpa Squirrel," called the smallest judge (who had the loudest voice).

The crowd on the green came across to look at the prize marrow. They all pushed to the front.

"Careful," called a judge. "You'll push the table over!" But it was too late. Over went the table, over went the judges, and a crowd of villagers fell kicking and squeaking on top of them.

"Ow!" squeaked Mr Weasel. "You're pricking me, Mr Prickles!" Just then there was a loud pop!

"What was that?" asked someone.

Mr Prickles crawled out from under the table and Grandpa shouted, "Look, everyone, look at that!"

Mr Prickles was covered in a huge burst balloon that had been painted with green stripes to look just like a marrow.

"It's Mr Weasel's marrow!" cried Little Squirrel. "He cheated."

Everyone looked round for Mr Weasel, but somehow he had managed to creep away without being seen.

"Congratulations," said Mr Bunny, patting Grandpa on the back. "First prize after all!"

Percy Woodpecker Makes Friends

"Today we're going to talk about rivers," said Mr Mole to the class and he wrote the word up on the board in blue chalk. While he was writing there was a tap, tap, tapping sound, but when Mr Mole turned round, no one was making a noise.

"I'd like you all . . ." began Mr Mole, but he stopped as the tap, tap, tap came again. "Quiet! Who is banging?" he asked.

No hands went up so Mr Mole carried on until the tapping started again and Little Squirrel, squealed, "Ow!"

"What is going on?" asked Mr Mole crossly.

It was Percy Woodpecker who had been tapping. He was a very

young woodpecker who had just started school. At the weekend his daddy had shown him how to peck holes in trees and it was such fun that Percy kept trying it out on everything. This time he had pecked through Little Squirrel's chair and pecked Little Squirrel too, by mistake!

"As you are new here, Percy," said Mr Mole, looking at the hole in the chair, "I won't get cross this time. But please, no more tapping."

Percy nodded and was very quiet for the rest of the lesson. He was rather shy, so at playtime he didn't go out to play with the others. He stayed inside and pecked a hole through Little Owl's ruler. Then he made a few holes in Little Squirrel's desk.

You can imagine how cross everybody was when they found out. Poor Percy couldn't understand what was wrong with making holes. They seemed nice to him, but nobody else liked them. He sat at his desk very quietly, feeling a bit sad.

The next lesson was painting and Mr Mole grumbled when he opened the cupboard and found the paintbrushes in a terrible mess. Some were stuck together, others were bent . . .

"It's disgraceful!" said Mr Mole as he handed them out.

Suddenly Percy had a good idea! It would make Mr Mole happy and maybe all the others would stop being cross too. He raced

home at lunchtime and ate his lunch so fast his mummy thought he would choke. Then he disappeared into the shed and all that could be heard for half an hour was tap, tap, tap.

"What *have* you made?" asked his mummy, looking at the square piece of wood with lots of holes. But Percy just grinned and ran off. He wanted to get back to school before anyone else.

When he reached the classroom, Percy opened the cupboard and took out all the paintbrushes. He popped them one by one into the holes in his piece of wood, then he put the new paintbrush-stand into the cupboard.

He just had time to sit down before everyone came running in. Mr Mole went to the cupboard to fetch the books and was very pleased when he saw how neat the paintbrushes were.

"I'm sorry I pecked holes in the wrong places," said Percy. "I'll only make useful ones from now on."

At playtime Benny Bunny asked Percy to make a hole in his conker. Very soon everyone was queuing up with conkers and Percy found he had made friends with them all.

Mrs Squirrel's Flowers

Mrs Squirrel liked to have a vase of flowers in the house. Every week she would go into the garden and pick a big bunch of whatever was in season. In the spring it might be daffodils or tulips. Now, in the autumn, it was chrysanthemums.

As she arranged her bunch of chrysanthemums one morning Mrs Squirrel sighed and looked sad.

"This is probably the last bunch of flowers I will pick in the garden before the snowdrops come up after Christmas," she told Little Squirrel. "I don't think a house looks quite as bright when there are no flowers in it."

Little Squirrel agreed. It would be nice to have bright flowers all year round. She would ask Grandpa Squirrel if there was any way it could be done; after all he knew all about growing flowers.

Grandpa said there were some special flowers called everlasting flowers which meant that they never died.

"We'll plant some next spring," he told her. "Then your mummy will have lovely flowers all through next winter."

"But that's no good for this winter," said Little Squirrel. "I'll have to think of something else."

Grandma Squirrel showed her some beautiful flowers made from silk that she had been given for her wedding.

"But I don't have any silk," said Little Squirrel.

She set off for home walking past the bare thorn hedge. Suddenly she saw a big blue flower on the hedge.

"How strange at this time of year," she thought, but when she got close to it she saw that it was a piece of blue paper. It gave Little Squirrel an idea.

As soon as she got home, Little Squirrel dashed up to her bedroom, and when she came down for lunch she had a lovely surprise for Mrs Squirrel—a big bunch of bright paper flowers.

"I made them from some wrapping paper we had left over from last Christmas," said Little Squirrel.

"How pretty," said her mummy. "Now I really can have flowers all year round!"

Mr Magpie to the Rescue

"What was that?" asked Mr Owl, sitting up in bed. He had been woken up by a loud squawking outside.

"It's only the neighbours," said Mrs Owl sleepily. The Owls lived next door to Mr and Mrs Magpie.

"I wish they wouldn't make so much noise so early in the morning," grumbled Mr Owl as he peered through the window. "And they ought to tidy up their place too. It's full of junk."

The Magpies weren't really untidy birds. They just couldn't help picking up anything bright and shiny which happened to be lying around. They had a huge collection of screws, teaspoons, hairpins and other odds and ends. Mr Magpie always thought they would come in useful one day, but they never seemed to. The pile outside their house just grew and grew.

"I'll make some tea, dear," said Mr Owl, with a yawn.

As he went downstairs he heard a strange, hissing sound. Mr Owl opened the kitchen door and saw a stream of water spurting from a hole in a pipe. The kitchen floor was awash!

Mr Owl rushed to the pipe and covered the hole with his wing.

"Help! Help!" he called, hoping that someone would hear.

Just then Mr Magpie flew by the window and, quick as a flash, he saw the problem.

"Hold on, Mr Owl," he called out. "I'll be back in a minute!"

Diving into his pile of screws and bolts, Mr Magpie chattered away to himself, "I knew it, I knew I'd use them one day!"

At last he found what he had been looking for and, gripping a big metal stopper tightly in his claws, he flew back to Mr Owl.

By now Mr Owl was knee-deep in water and he was very glad to see Mr Magpie. Together they managed to wiggle the stopper into the hole—and the water stopped.

Mr Owl felt tired and wobbly.

"Thank you, Mr Magpie," he said as he mopped his feathers dry.

That evening as Mr and Mrs Owl sat together by the fire, they decided that they had the very best of neighbours.

"You see, dear," said Mr Owl, "all those odds and ends that the Magpies collect might look a bit untidy, but you never know when something will come in useful."

The Treasure Hunt

It was Little Bunny's birthday, but Mrs Bunny wouldn't tell him or his friends where the party was to be.

"You'll have to find out," she explained. "Follow the clues and they will lead you to the party." She read out the first clue.

I'm the oldest tree,
You can learn a lot of things from me.

"The oldest tree in our village is the oak!" shouted Little Owl.

"And you learn a lot in school," added Little Squirrel.

They ran to the school and found the next clue pinned to the oak tree in the playground.

In the stream we stand high
To keep your feet dry.

"I know what it means!" shouted Little Bunny, excitedly.

"What?" they all cried, but he ran off calling, "You've got to work it out!"

Suddenly Timmy Mouse said, "It must be the stepping stones!" and they all headed for the stream. Little Bunny had already found the clue and gone on to the next one.

"Here's the clue," said Little Squirrel.

Look out for a bright blue door,
You'll find buns to eat and much, much more.

"Who's got a bright blue door?" asked Little Owl.

"The Bunnies!" called Nippy Shrew. "Their front door is blue and there'll be lots of lovely things to eat because it's a party!"

"Well done! You got here quickly," said Mrs Bunny when they ran in at the garden gate. "But where's Little Bunny?"

They were all puzzled. Little Bunny was ahead of them so he should have got there first.

Mr Bunny thought it served Little Bunny right for not helping the others with the clue, but he said he would go to look for him anyway.

As he walked into the village Mr Bunny could see Mrs Prickles the baker, wagging her finger at Little Bunny!

"Oh dear, I wonder what's wrong," thought Mr Bunny.

Then he noticed that Mrs Prickles had a bright blue front door, just like their own. Little Bunny was standing beside it looking very sorry for himself.

"I'm glad you're here, Mr Bunny,' said Mrs Prickles. "This young bunny seems to think I'm having a party here, which I'm not. And he seems to think these buns are his, which they aren't!"

Mr Bunny laughed. "You've got the wrong blue door, Little Bunny. Have you forgotten that our front door is blue too? There are already some buns for you at home, but I'd like to buy a few more, if you've some to spare, Mrs Prickles."

"Of course," said Mrs Prickles, smiling now. And, carrying a bag of buns between them, Mr Bunny and Little Bunny hurried home to the party.

The School Outing

One fine spring morning there was a lot of noise in the playground at Hollyholt School. Everyone was excited. There were to be no lessons at all today. They were going on a school trip.

The coach arrived and they all scrambled on clutching their picnic lunches. Soon they were out of the village and driving through open countryside, past fields of hay and barley, then along beside a river, until at last they climbed up and up a steep hill on top of which stood Bilberry Castle.

Mr Mole led them round and told them all about the castle.

"This is where the Bilberry Bunnies lived," he said. "We are standing in the Great Hall where they held feasts that lasted a week with dancing and music and games. Let's go up to the bedroom and see the old beds that they once slept in."

"What funny beds!" said Little Squirrel. "They've all got curtains round them."

"I think it's a good idea," said Percy Woodpecker. "Keeps you warm in winter."

"They're very lumpy," called Little Owl.

"You aren't supposed to climb on them," said Mr Mole. "Off!"

Next they visited the armoury where the old Knights of Bilberry Castle stored their swords and suits of armour.

"Imagine what it was like wearing a heavy iron suit like this," said Mr Mole.

Last of all they climbed the tower.

"Look, there's the river!" cried Little Owl. "Isn't it a long way down?"

"Time to go," said Mr Mole.

Everyone hurried back to the coach. Mr Mole stood by the door and counted them as they got in.

"We're one short," he said when everyone had sat down. "Who's missing?"

"It's Percy," called Little Owl. "Percy's missing."

"Little Mouse, would you mind going back to fetch him?" asked Mr Mole.

Little Mouse ran back to the castle.

A few minutes later she returned running as fast as she could, quite out of breath and with no sign of Percy Woodpecker.

"What *is* the matter?" asked Mr Mole.

"G-g-ghost! I've seen a ghost!" she whispered. "It was wearing a suit of armour—just like the ones we saw."

"I think we'd *all* better go and look for Percy," said Mr Mole.

They walked slowly into the castle. As they got near to the armoury they could hear a noise. Little Mouse peered round the door and saw one of the suits of armour shaking from side to side and rattling as it did so. Mr Mole suddenly laughed.

"That's no ghost!" he said aloud and walked right up to the shaking figure.

He lifted the helmet off and there was Percy Woodpecker trying very hard to get out of the suit of armour that he had tried on!

Mrs Mouse Loses Her Ring

It was baking day in the Mouse house and Mrs Mouse was making scones, biscuits and some crusty loaves of bread. She put the last loaf into the oven and then put the kettle on to make a cup of tea.

"You sit down. I'll make it," said Mr Mouse and Mrs Mouse propped herself up comfortably on the sofa.

"My hands are tired from kneading all that bread," she said, stretching them out. Then she noticed that her ring was missing.

It wasn't on the windowsill (where she usually left it) and it wasn't on the table where she had been working. Timmy and Mr

Mouse joined the search and they hunted all over the kitchen. Timmy ran upstairs to see if she had left it in the bedroom. It wasn't there either.

"I've lost my ring," said Mrs Mouse, who was almost crying.

"Don't worry," said Mr Mouse putting his arm round her. "It's bound to turn up. Perhaps you dropped it in the dough while you were making the bread."

"That's it!" said Mrs Mouse. "I was wearing it when I started baking, so I must have dropped it in the dough! The only problem is which loaf? Or it could be in one of the scones."

"We'll just have to eat them until we find it," said Mr Mouse. "I know, let's invite some friends to tea to help."

At teatime there was quite a crowd round the Mouse family's kitchen table and Mr Mouse sliced up loaf after loaf to feed everyone. They finished all the bread, but there was no sign of Mrs Mouse's ring.

"We'd better eat the scones. It's bound to be in one of those," said Mr Mouse, handing the plate round.

The scones were nearly gone and still there was no sign of the missing ring. Mrs Mouse started to worry, but she tried not to show it.

"Would anyone like another cup of tea?" she asked. "Oh dear, we're running out of milk," she said, tipping the milk jug right up.

As she did so there was a little rattle and something fell into the teacup. It was the missing ring!

Everyone began to laugh. "We've just eaten a whole week's baking to find that," said Mr Mouse. "And it was in the milk jug all the time!"

Carol Singing

"Let's go carol singing this Christmas," suggested Little Squirrel.

"That sounds like a good idea," said Little Mouse, and several others asked if they could come.

Soon Little Squirrel had quite a group of singers.

"We'll meet at my house for a practice on Tuesday," said Little Squirrel and she handed them sheets with the words on so they could learn the carols.

At the practice they all started to sing loudly with Little Squirrel conducting them. She couldn't help noticing that someone was singing out of tune. It was Little Owl.

"What can we do?" she asked Little Mouse afterwards. "He can't sing in tune and he'll spoil the whole thing, but I don't want to upset him by telling him that."

"I expect he'll get better when we've practised a bit more," said Little Mouse. "Don't worry about it."

But Little Owl didn't get better. In fact, as everyone else got better, Little Owl's singing could be heard even more clearly.

"What you need to do," suggested Little Bunny, "is give him a job. Maybe he could collect the money or knock on doors."

"But he will still sing while he does it," pointed out Little Mouse.

"You've just given me an idea, Little Bunny," said Little Squirrel and she dashed off.

42

When the carol singing night arrived they all gathered outside Little Squirrel's house, warmly wrapped up in scarves and gloves, for it was cold and snowy.

"Little Owl," said Little Squirrel, "please will you carry the lantern to light our way?"

Little Owl was very pleased that she had asked him. The lantern was a night light in a little jar without a top to it and he had to carry it very carefully to make sure it didn't go out.

They arrived at the Bunnies' house and started to sing. Little Owl took a deep breath and sang one note. As he did so he blew out the night light.

He had to ask Mr Bunny to relight it for him and then he decided that he had better not sing, just in case he did it again. After all, carrying the lantern was a much more important job!

Grandpa's Magnifying Glass

Grandpa Squirrel's eyes weren't too good, so he used a magnifying glass to read with. Every morning, when he had finished pottering in the garden he would settle down in his favourite armchair with the newspaper and his magnifying glass.

Little Squirrel loved peering through the glass as it made everything look much bigger, just like magic!

One morning when she was staying at Grandpa and Grandma Squirrel's she had an idea.

"Wouldn't it be wonderful to take the magnifying glass into the garden and look at all sorts of tiny things—blades of grass, tiny insects, the seed-heads of flowers?—I'm sure Grandpa won't mind," she thought.

On this particular morning Grandpa stayed in bed late so Little Squirrel couldn't ask him, but she helped herself to the glass and went out to look at cobwebs and things.

When Grandpa got up he thought he would read the paper, but of course he couldn't find his glass.

"Perhaps I didn't put it away yesterday," he said and he began to hunt all round the room.

Grandma joined in too and they both hunted everywhere. They were still hunting for it when Little Squirrel came running in from the garden.

"There it is!" cried Grandpa. "What were you doing with my glass, you naughty Little Squirrel?"

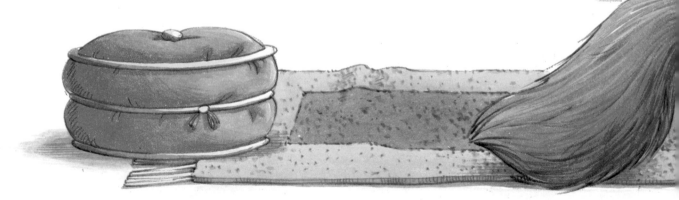

44

"I only wanted to make tiny things in the garden look bigger," said Little Squirrel. "I'm sorry, Grandpa. I found something in the grass too," she told them and held out her paw.

"Why, it's my earring!" said Grandma in surprise. "I lost it last week when we were out in the garden. I've been looking for it ever since!"

"Well done, sharp eyes," said Grandpa, who had stopped feeling cross. "You can borrow my glass whenever you like—so long as you ask first! Perhaps we'll find a whole treasure trove in the garden," he added with a wink.